BARNYARD BANTER

FOR LAURA GODWIN,
MY BANTERING BUDDY

1 3 5 7 9 10 8 6 4 2

Copyright © Denise Fleming 1994

Denise Fleming has asserted her right under the Copyright,
Designs and Patents Act, 1988 to be identified as the author and
illustrator of this work

First published in the United Kingdom 1994
by The Bodley Head Children's Books
Random House, 20 Vauxhall Bridge Road
London, SW1V 2SA

First published in the USA by Henry Holt and Company 1994

Random House UK Limited Reg. No. 954009

A CIP catalogue record for this book is available from the British
Library

ISBN 0 370 31931 1

Printed in China

BARNYARD BANTER

Denise Fleming

The Bodley Head • London

Cows in the pasture,
moo,
moo,
moo

Roosters in the barnyard,

cock-a-doodle-doo

Hens in the henhouse,

cluck,

cluck,

cluck

Pigs in the wallow,

muck,

muck,

muck

But where's Goose?

Kittens in the hayloft,

mew, mew, mew, mew

Pigeons
in the rafters,

COO, COO,
COO

Mice
in the grain bin,

squeak,

squeak,

Peacocks in the wire pen,

Donkeys in the paddock,

Crows
in the cornfield,

caw,

caw,

caw

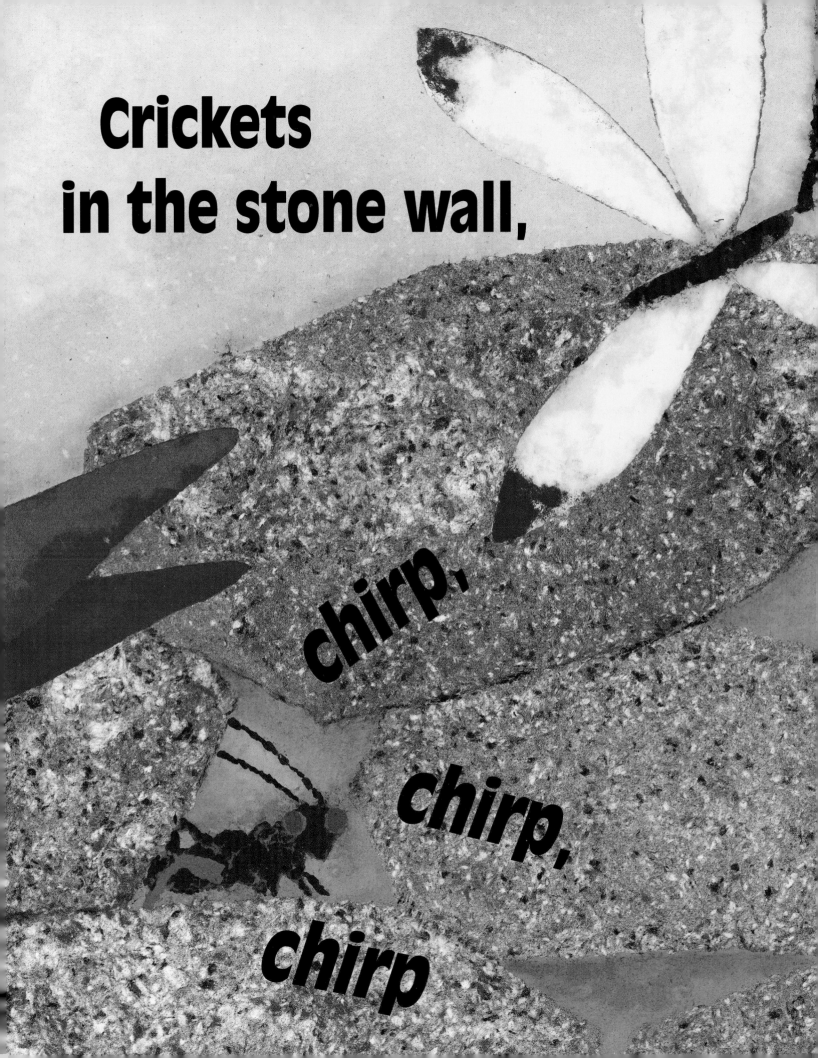

Crickets
in the stone wall,

chirp,

chirp,

chirp

Frogs
in the farm pond,

moo, moo, moo

cock -a- doodle -doo

cluck, cluck, cluck

muck, muck, muck

mew, mew, mew   coo, coo,
coo

squeak, squeak, squeak

shriek, shriek,
shriek

hee, haw, haw

caw, caw, caw

chirp, chirp, chirp

burp, burp, burp

But where's
Goose?

There's Goose!

honk,

honk,

honk,

honk